RED LIGHT
GREEN LIGHT

WRITTEN BY GOLDEN MacDONALD

ILLUSTRATED BY LEONARD WEISGARD

DOUBLEDAY & COMPANY, INC., GARDEN CITY, NEW YORK

40713

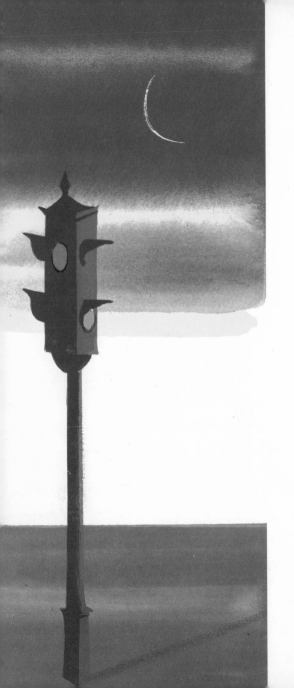

RED LIGHT

GREEN LIGHT

GOOD MORNING

doubleday

3·08

3-6-68

STOP

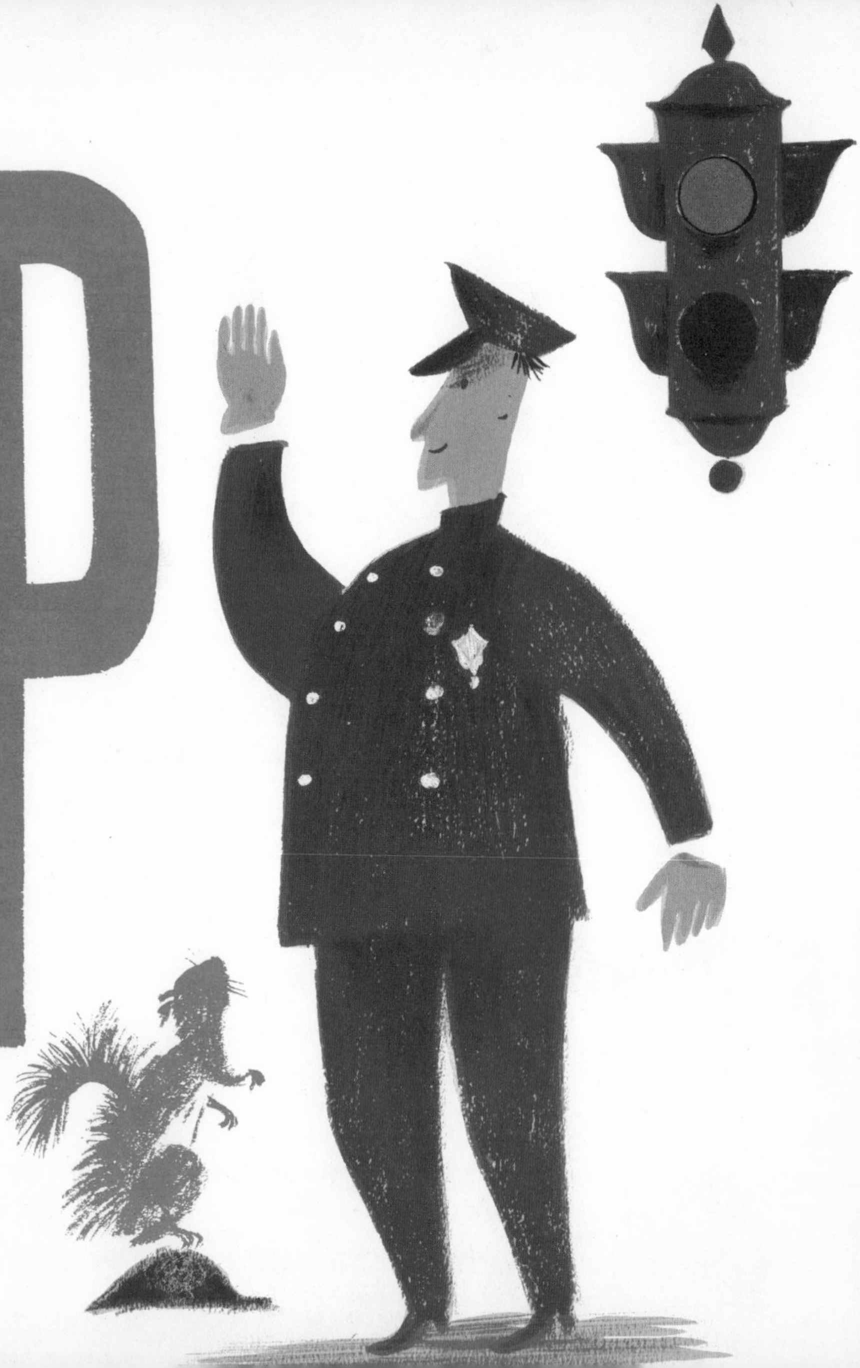

In the morning they all came out of their houses.

Red Light they can't go.

Green Light they can go.

The truck came out of the truck's house
a garage.

The car came out of the car's house
another garage.

The jeep came out of the jeep's house
a tent.

The horse came out of the horse's house
a barn.

The boy came out of the boy's house

a home.

The dog came out of the dog's house

a kennel.

The cat climbed down from the cat's house

a tree.

(This was a wild cat.)

And the mouse came out of the house of the mouse

a hole.

Red Light they can't go.
Green Light they can.

And they all went down their own roads.
Truck and car and bicycle and horse roads
Jeep roads across fields

Dog roads
Cat roads
And mouse roads through the grass.

Green Light they can go.
Red Light they can't.

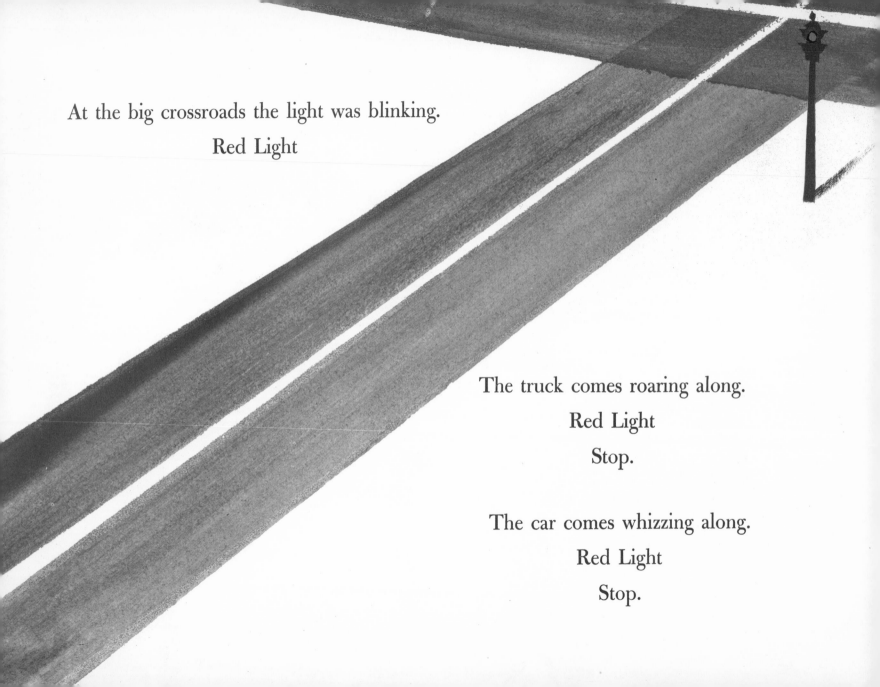

At the big crossroads the light was blinking.
Red Light

The truck comes roaring along.
Red Light
Stop.

The car comes whizzing along.
Red Light
Stop.

The jeep comes jeeping along.

Red Light

Stop.

The horse comes trotting along.

Red Light

Stop.

The cat comes creeping along.

Red Light

Stop.

RED LIGHT

The mouse came along.
Red Light a bunny's eyes.
Green Light a cat's.

STOP

GREEN LIGHT

GO

Green Light they did go.
Red Light they didn't.

They went around all day until it was night.

Then all the lights turned on along the
roads and in the houses because it was night.
And they all went home.

Red Light they didn't go.
Green Light they did.

The truck went into the truck's house

a garage.

The car went into the car's house

another garage.

The jeep went into the jeep's house

a tent.

The horse went into the horse's house

a barn.

The boy went into the boy's house

a home.

The dog went into the dog's house

a kennel.

The cat went into the cat's house

a tree.

(This was a wild cat.)

And the mouse crept into the house of the mouse

a hole.

Red Light they can't go.
Green Light they can.

All things were asleep.

Through holes and doors and windows
lights blinked off
Until there was only a Red Light
and a Green Light
blinking in the darkness.

RED LIGHT

GREEN LIGHT

GOOD NIGHT